*For John Kaufman — S.K.*
*To Mike, Sue, Molly and John — N.D.*

Library of Congress Cataloging in Publication Data
Kroll, Steven.  Otto.

Summary: Otto the robot accompanies his small friend
to school and ends up being chased by the entire class when
he runs away with their juice.

[1. Stories in rhyme.  2. Robots—Fiction.  3. School Stories]
I. Delaney, Ned, ill.  II. Title.
PZ8.3.K8990t  1983  [E]  82-19042
ISBN 0-8193-1105-7
ISBN 0-8193-1106-5 (lib. bdg.)

A Parents Magazine
READ ALOUD AND EASY READING PROGRAM® Original.

Distributed in Canada by Clarke, Irwin & Co., Ltd.
Toronto, Canada

# OTTO

## by Steven Kroll
## pictures by Ned Delaney

**Parents Magazine Press** • **New York**

Otto is
A robot
Living in
My house.

Otto sleeps
Beside me
Quiet as
A mouse.

AMPHIBIAN...

But at half
Past seven
Otto gets
Right up.

Otto shakes
My blanket
Otto says
"Beep, bup!"

Jump up from
The covers
Quickly fill
The tub.

Otto keeps
Me going
Otto helps
Me scrub.

Then we have
Our breakfast
Otto makes
Us toast.

Next I oil
His gearbox
Where he needs
It most.

When we reach
Our classroom
All the kids
Say "Hi!"

Otto looks
So happy
"Beep, bup" he
Replies.

Teacher asks
A question
Otto's arm
Goes up.

Teacher says
"Yes, Otto"
Otto says
"Beep, bup!"

All his lights
Flash on and
Something turns
His gears.

Circuits pop
Levers drop
Then a card
Appears.

Otto has
The answer
Otto knows
His stuff.

He stands up
And dances
Till he starts
To puff.

Puff and puff
Goes Otto
Now he starts
To spin.

Something's wrong
With Otto
See the shape
He's in.

Otto finds
A broom and
Starts to sweep
The door.

Then jumps on
A desk and
Starts to sweep
Some more.

After that
He tries some
Cartwheels for
A while.

But he just
Can't make them
Tumbles in
A pile.

He is just
So silly
What could have
Gone wrong?

Teacher asks
"What's happened?"
Otto says
"Greep, grong!"

Once again
His lights start
Winking off
And on.

Otto grabs
The juice tray
In a flash
He's gone!

No one can
Believe he's
Taken all
Our juice.

"Catch him!" says
Our teacher
"He is on
The loose."

Up the stairs
We chase him
Then we chase
Him down.

Out into
The yard and
Out around
The town.

Finally
He leads us
Right back in
To class.

Not a drop
Of juice has
Spilled from cup
Or glass.

"What is wrong?"
We ask him
Otto makes
A face.

Circuits pop
Levers drop
Then a card's
In place.

I pull out
My oil can
Oil from head
To toes.

Otto smiles
And wiggles
And his top
Light glows!

Happy now
He serves us
Each a glass
Or cup.

Otto's lights
Go flashing...

Otto says
"Beep, bup!"

## About the Author and Artist

STEVEN KROLL is the author of many popular books for children, including *The Goat Parade,* published by Parents. The idea for *Otto* came to him one day as he sat enjoying a sunny afternoon in an outdoor cafe in New York City. "I had often wondered what it would be like if robots really came to live with us. Not very friendly, I thought. So I tried to imagine a robot that was something like a person and *was* friendly. At that moment Otto was born."

NED DELANEY has been writing and illustrating picture books since he graduated from college. He also teaches writing and illustrating at Salem State College in the Boston area, where he lives. Mr. Delaney says that some of his ideas for Otto came from studying household appliances, such as his lawnmower and toaster. "But Otto's head is my tribute to the Tin Man," says Mr. Delaney.